White-Water Kayaking

By Mike Graf

Consultant:
Brian Parsons
Director of Slalom
USA Canoe/Kayak
Charlotte, North Carolina

Capstone
press

Mankato, Minnesota

Capstone High-Interest Books are published by Capstone Press
151 Good Counsel Drive, P.O. Box 669, Mankato, Minnesota 56002
www.capstonepress.com

Library of Congress Cataloging-in-Publication Data
Graf, Mike
    White-water kayaking/by Mike Graf.
    p. cm.—(The great outdoors)
    Includes bibliographical references and index (p. 48).
    ISBN 0-7368-2413-8
    1. Kayaking—Juvenile literature. [1. White-water canoeing 2. Kayaks and
kayaking.]
I. Title. II. Series.
GV784.3 .G73 2004
797.1'224—dc22   2003018354

Summary: Describes the equipment, skills, conservation issues, and safety concerns
of white-water kayaking.

Editorial Credits
James Anderson, editor; Timothy Halldin, series designer; Molly Nei,
    book designer and illustrator; Jo Miller, photo researcher

Photo Credits
Capstone Press/Gary Sundermeyer, cover (inset), 21, 25, 29, 40 (all)
Corbis, 7; Charlie Munsey, 39; Gary Braasch, 30; Mark Gamba, cover (bottom)
Diane Meyer, 4, 13, 26
Folio Inc./Rob Crandall, cover (top)
Getty Images/Shaun Botterill, 8
Larry Prosor, 10, 14, 18
Photodisc Inc., 1, 43
UNICORN Stock Photos/Jeff Greenberg, 22; Robert W. Ginn, 35; Robin Rudd,
    17, 36

Capstone Press thanks Steve Herbeck for his help with this book.

1 2 3 4 5 6 09 08 07 06 05 04

Table of Contents

CHAPTER 1

White-Water Kayaking

A kayaker visiting the northwestern United States races over river rapids in her brightly colored kayak. She is part of a wildwater race. As she reaches a small drop-off in the water, the kayak bounces in the river with its front pointed at the sky.

After a hard day of racing, the kayaker camps for the night. Before she camps, she ties her kayak to a tree along the river.

First Kayaks

Native people of the Arctic first used kayaks. Siberia, Greenland, and northern North America make up this region. The kayaks were used for hunting seals and whales and for fishing.

Some kayakers do tricks while racing down rivers.

People from the Arctic made the frame of their kayaks from wood or animal bone. They stretched sealskin over the frame. Arctic people stayed warm and dry inside the sealskin kayaks while traveling on rivers and in the ocean.

The native people of Alaska are called Inuit. They named their boats *qayaq*. This word means "hunter's boat." Inuit hunters paddled their *qayaqs* in the Arctic water to find large animals. The *qayaqs* were lightweight enough for Inuits to carry over frozen water.

Kayaks in Europe

Europeans visited Alaska in the 1700s. They brought *qayaqs* back to Europe. People in Europe changed the spelling to kayak.

In the early 1900s, German and French boat builders copied the kayak style. They built kayaks for people to paddle on mountain rivers.

Inuit hunters used *qayaqs* to reach seals and whales.

Soon, kayaks were used in the United States and Canada. People used the kayaks to travel quickly on fast-moving rivers.

White-Water Kayaks

In the 1950s, boat makers in the United States began to make fiberglass kayaks. Fiberglass kayaks are stronger and less likely to be damaged in rough water.

Slalom kayakers race between poles on a river.

Today, kayaks are made from many
materials. Some kayaks are inflatable.
People use air to blow up these plastic kayaks.
Kayaks used in white-water races are made of
stronger materials such as carbon and Kevlar.

Competitions

Slalom is the most popular type of kayak race. These races take place on fast-moving stretches of river. Two wood poles hang from ropes strung across the river. Slalom kayakers need to go between the poles during the race.

Slalom races last less than two minutes. The fastest kayakers receive the best scores. Kayakers are also judged on how well they control their boat.

Wildwater racing is popular. Experienced kayakers race over courses on quickly moving rivers. The courses are about 2 miles (3.2 kilometers) long.

Another type of competition is called freestyle. Freestyle kayakers do tricks with their boats. They tip their kayaks from front to back on the water. They also bounce their boats on the bows and sterns for several seconds. Some tricks are performed in small kayaks called "squirt boats." Freestyle judges give kayakers good scores for original and exciting tricks.

CHAPTER 2

Equipment

Kayakers must prepare for dangerous adventures. Training is a big part of being prepared. Kayakers also need proper equipment before they hit the water.

Kayaks

White-water kayaks are designed for use on river adventures. They are easy to carry in and out of the water. An average kayak weighs 30 pounds (14 kilograms). Kayaks can be from 6 to 18 feet (2 to 6 meters) long. The long, narrow shape of kayaks helps them glide over rapids.

Kayaks are lightweight, so kayakers can carry them over land.

Kayakers sit in a hole in the center of the boat. This area is called the cockpit. Most kayaks are made for only one person. Some kayaks have two-person cockpits.

A spray skirt fits around the cockpit to keep the inside of the kayak dry. This skirt is made of rubber. Kayakers wear the skirt around the waist. The skirt fits tightly over kayakers' clothing. Kayakers stretch the skirt around the opening of the cockpit after they sit in their kayak.

Spray skirts have an automatic release line. The spray skirt releases from the kayak when the line is pulled. Kayakers pull this line if they flip their kayak and cannot roll it back to the upright position. The spray skirt then separates from the kayak, allowing the kayaker to swim to safety. Kayakers swim to shore if water conditions are rough. If the water is calm, kayakers swim back to their kayak.

A spray skirt keeps water from entering the kayak.

Paddles

Kayakers control the kayak with paddles. Kayaking paddles have two blades. The blades can be made of wood or plastic. Some blades are made of carbon and Kevlar. Paddles with these strong blades are most often used for white-water kayaking.

The shaft of the paddle is the middle tube that connects the blades. Shafts are made of wood, fiberglass, or aluminum. Many shafts have rubber hand areas where kayakers can grip the paddle.

A paddle of proper length is important to white-water kayakers. White-water and wildwater kayakers use paddles that are about one arm's length longer than the kayaker's height. Freestyle or squirt kayakers use shorter paddles. Short paddles allow these kayakers to make quick turns in their kayaks.

Squirt kayakers use short paddles to make quick turns.

Life Jacket

Kayakers often call life jackets personal flotation devices, or PFDs. These vests are necessary for kayaking.

PFDs keep kayakers afloat if they fall into the water. A properly fitting PFD keeps a person's nose and mouth out of the water. PFDs come in a variety of styles, sizes, and colors. Kayakers wear PFDs in both calm and fast water.

Helmet

Helmets are important to white-water kayakers. Kayak helmets are made of hard plastic. The helmets are padded with foam. Straps hold the helmets in place. Some helmets cover a kayaker's ears. Others are cut above the ears so that they do not block a kayaker's hearing.

Extra protection can be added to helmets. Some kayakers add a chin bar or a wire face cage. These items prevent a kayaker's face

A helmet helps protect a kayaker from injury.

from scraping against rocks in the water if the boat is overturned.

Other Items

Other equipment helps white-water kayakers. Kayakers who ride in cold weather often use extra equipment.

Paddle jackets keep kayakers' upper bodies warm and dry. The jackets are made of waterproof materials. The neck and cuffs of the jacket are designed to keep out water. Kayakers buy paddle jackets that are lightweight and roomy. Comfortable jackets allow kayakers to move their arms freely when paddling.

Kayaking gloves are made to grip a paddle. They also keep a kayaker's hands dry and warm. Some gloves have fingers. Fingerless gloves improve grip, but they do not keep kayakers' fingers as warm.

Pogies attach to the paddle and serve as protection for a kayaker's hands. Kayakers wear pogies like mittens. Pogies keep kayakers' hands warm during cold weather.

Kayakers also wear wetsuit boots in cold weather. These boots are waterproof. They slip over kayakers' shoes and keep their feet warm and dry.

Kayakers wear equipment that keeps them dry.

Float bags protect kayakers who flip. Kayakers fill these bags with air and tuck them inside their kayaks. Most kayaks have room for a float bag in the front and the back of the boat. Float bags help keep the kayak afloat so that kayakers can easily climb back into the boat after an accident.

Kayakers use throw ropes to tie kayaks to a tree on shore. Throw ropes are helpful when kayakers stop to camp for the night. Kayakers also use ropes to tie boats together. Kayakers may also use throw ropes to rescue people who have fallen into the water.

wet suit

rope

paddle

white-water kayak

spray skirt

PFD

float bags

helmet

granola bars

water bottle

gloves

Equipment

- float bags
- gloves
- granola bars
- helmet
- paddle
- PFD (personal floatation device)
- rope
- spray skirt
- water bottle
- wet suit
- white-water kayak

21

CHAPTER 3

White-Water Techniques

Kayakers must be good swimmers. Even with PFDs, kayakers need to be able to swim back to their boats or to shore.

Lessons

White-water kayakers should take kayaking lessons from an experienced instructor. Beginning kayakers usually learn to paddle a kayak in a swimming pool or in calm water. They also practice advanced moves in calm water. Later, the instructor takes the kayaker to a river to practice in moving water.

Beginning kayakers receive lessons from an instructor.

Forward Stroke

The forward stroke is the most basic kayaking stroke. Paddlers use this stroke to move the kayak forward in the water.

To do a forward stroke, the paddler sits with the chest forward and the chin up. The kayaker holds the paddle in front of the body. The paddler turns so that one blade of the paddle is ahead of the other. The kayaker then puts the front blade in the water and moves the blade alongside the boat.

As the paddle moves through the water, the kayak moves forward. The kayaker continues switching from right to left with each stroke.

Backstroke

The backstroke is the opposite of the forward stroke. Kayakers push the back blade away from them during a backstroke. When kayakers push on the blade, the kayak moves backward.

Kayaker Diagram

helmet

grip

shaft

blade

personal
flotation device

This stroke is useful when a kayaker wants to avoid trouble ahead. The backstroke helps kayakers move the boat away from rocks, trees, or other dangerous objects in the river.

A kayaker turns upside down and back to the upright position during an Eskimo roll.

Turning Stroke

Kayakers also use the turning stroke to avoid objects on a river. To turn the kayak to the right, the paddler moves the left blade of the paddle to the front. With the left blade of the paddle in the water, the kayaker pushes the paddle outward, away from the boat.

To turn the kayak to the left, the kayaker moves the right blade of the paddle to the front. The kayaker places the right blade of the paddle in the water and pushes the paddle away from the boat.

Eskimo Roll

In rough water, kayaks can flip. Kayakers can do an Eskimo roll to turn the boat back to the upright position. This move is named for Inuit kayakers who were once called Eskimos. An Eskimo roll moves kayakers from upright to upside down and back to the upright position.

Kayakers swoop at the water with their paddle while turning their bodies during this move. Kayakers gain speed from the movement of their body and the paddle and push the kayak back to the upright position.

Wet Exit

Kayakers also can do a wet exit. While the kayak is upside down, paddlers pull the release cord to remove the spray skirt from the cockpit.

If the water is calm, paddlers may try to turn their kayaks upright and continue down the river. In rough water, kayakers quickly swim to shore.

Advanced Techniques

Experienced kayakers do advanced moves. Advanced moves include the draw stroke and the eddy turn.

The draw stroke can move a kayak sideways down a river. Kayakers use this move instead of a backstroke to steer kayaks around obstacles. White-water kayakers use this stroke because it allows them to keep up their speed.

An eddy turn can move a boat from fast to calm water. An eddy is a circular current in the water. Eddies often form as water rushes around a boulder. Kayaks turn as they hit the rushing water after a boulder. Kayakers lean into the turn. They paddle to the calm area behind the boulder.

Trail Mix

Ingredients:
raisins
peanuts
cashews
candy coated chocolate pieces

Equipment:
mixing bowl
sealable plastic bags
spoon

What You Do:
1. Put a handful of each ingredient in the bowl.
2. Mix everything together with the spoon.
3. Put some of the mixture into a plastic bag and seal it so it stays dry.

CHAPTER 4

Conservation

Responsible white-water kayakers want to keep rivers clean. Many paddlers have formed groups that preserve rivers and protect them from erosion and pollution.

Erosion

Weathering causes erosion. Weathering occurs when rock and soil break down. Soil often breaks down due to flooding caused by rain or melting snow. The flooded river sweeps away broken-down soil.

Erosion changes the shape of a river. Kayakers need to know how to move through an eroded area. They need to stay near the center of the river. The outside of an eroded river bend is often dangerous. Paddlers watch for strainers, such as small brush and exposed trees, in these areas.

Erosion causes rivers to change shape and speed.

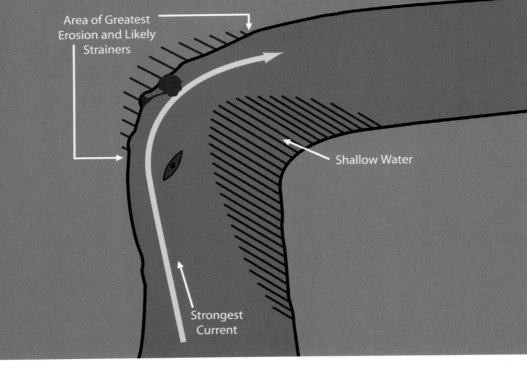

Erosion Diagram

Area of Greatest Erosion and Likely Strainers

Shallow Water

Strongest Current

To help control erosion, conservation groups plant grasses and trees and place large boulders along rivers. The roots of these plants and the weight of the boulders hold the soil in place.

White-water kayakers pay close attention to erosion. They take action when erosion is discovered in an area. The sooner that grasses and trees are planted, the sooner an area of river can again be safe for kayakers.

Pollution

Pollutants in the air and land cause most river pollution. Air polluted by a mixture of fog and smoke is called smog. Rain falls through smog and lands on the ground.

Polluted rain that falls to the ground later flows into rivers. The rain water picks up polluted dirt, sand, and other particles as it flows over land.

Clean Water Act

The U.S. Congress passed the Clean Water Act (CWA) in 1972. This federal law says that state and national government groups are responsible for finding sources of pollution.

Since the CWA was passed, many pollution sources have been discovered and fixed. City sewer plants are no longer able to dump waste into local rivers.

Because of the CWA, many groups have formed to help solve the world's pollution problems. White-water kayakers are often members of these groups. They work to keep the rivers clean.

State and Local Laws

Cities, counties, and states have laws about conservation and pollution. Most vehicles need pollution control parts. Many city, county, and state parks have litter laws to protect nearby rivers.

Everyone must understand pollution laws. Business people and farmers need to prevent pollution. People who notice illegal pollution should report it to authorities.

Factory waste pollutes rivers.

CHAPTER 5

Safety

Most white-water paddlers begin kayaking lessons on calm rivers and lakes. As they learn beginning paddling techniques, they become comfortable with their kayaks. Beginning paddlers also learn the safety tips that are necessary for white-water paddling.

Weather

Paddlers listen to weather forecasts before kayaking. Weather can change quickly. A prepared kayaker is aware of weather changes that may occur.

During rain, the water in a river can rise to dangerous levels. Rivers with high water levels move fast. White-water kayakers are prepared for fast-moving water. They do not kayak on rivers if heavy rain is expected.

Kayaking events are held in good weather.

Kayakers are also aware of possible dangers under the water. A fallen tree may be easy to avoid when water levels are low. At a high water level, the tree may be hidden. If kayaks were to hit an object under water, the boats could flip or become damaged.

Scouting

Kayakers know the importance of seeing any problems that lie ahead on a river. When kayakers scout, they look ahead to see what obstacles are coming.

Scouting is done from the kayak or from shore. Drops and rapids can be fun, but they are also dangerous. White-water kayakers sometimes carry their kayaks around rough areas. Kayakers scout for these areas so they have time to get their boats safely to shore.

Kayakers can handle dangerous areas when they know what is ahead of them.

Universal River Signals

Kayakers use river signals to communicate with others. These signals help keep kayakers safe on rivers.

Stop

Kayakers use this signal if they want other kayakers to stop. They stretch their arms above their head and hold the paddle to form a "T."

Help/Emergency

Kayakers make this signal if they need help. Paddlers wave the paddle over their heads and blow 3 long blasts on a whistle.

All Clear

This signal tells other kayakers that the river is safe ahead. Kayakers hold the paddle straight up to tell others to move ahead on the river.

Safety Signals

White-water kayakers know the universal river signals. This set of arm movements was designed for easy communication on rivers.

Each signal has a meaning. Common signals are "stop," "help," and "all clear."

Future of White-Water Kayaking

White-water kayaking is a sport that people of all ages can enjoy. Experienced paddlers share their knowledge with others who are learning to kayak so that white-water kayaking will continue to become more popular.

Whether for adventure or competition, white-water kayakers enjoy their sport. An interest in conservation and safety helps white-water kayakers promote their sport as a good way to experience and enjoy the outdoors.

International Scale of River Difficulty

Class I
Moving water. Small ripples or waves. Few or no obstacles.

Class II
Easy rapids with waves as high as 3 feet (1 meter). Wide, clear channels. Some boat steering may be needed. Kayaks could tip or be swamped by waves.

Class III
Long, difficult rapids and passages. Experienced moves are needed in rough waters. Scouting ahead from shore is necessary. Rescue is difficult in this water. Boaters should know how to do the Eskimo roll.

Class IV
Extremely difficult, long, and violent rapids. Boaters must scout the river ahead of time. Rescue would be very difficult.

Class V
Nearly impossible waters and very dangerous. For experts only.

Glossary

aluminum (uh-LOO-mi-nuhm)—a lightweight, silver-colored metal

bow (BOU)—the front of a boat

conservation (kon-sur-VAY-shuhn)—the protection of rivers, forests, and other natural resources

fiberglass (FYE-bur-glass)—a strong material made from fine threads of glass

forecast (FORE-kast)—a prediction of things that will happen, such as weather conditions

Kevlar (KEV-lahr)—a material made of strong artificial fibers

pogies (PO-gees)—mitts that kayakers wear; pogies attach to the paddle and keep the kayakers' hands warm.

pollution (puh-LOO-shuhn)—harmful materials that damage or contaminate the environment

stern (STERN)—the back of a boat

Read More

Bach, Julie S. *Kayaking.* World of Sports. Mankato, Minn.: Smart Apple Media, 2001.

Jackson, Eric. *Whitewater Paddling: Strokes and Concepts.* Mechanicsberg, Penn.: Stackpole Books, 1999.

Useful Addresses

American Whitewater
1424 Fenwick Lane
Silver Spring, MD 20910

Canadian Canoe Association
2197 Riverside Drive
Suite 705
Ottawa, Ontario K1H 7X3

**Leave No Trace Center
   for Outdoor Ethics**
P.O. Box 997
Boulder, CO 80306

USA Canoe/Kayak
230 South Tryon Street
Suite 220
Charlotte, NC 28202

Internet Sites

FactHound offers a safe, fun way to find Internet sites related to this book. All of the sites on FactHound have been researched by our staff.

Here's how:
1. Visit *www.facthound.com*
2. Type in this special code
   0736824138 for age-appropriate sites. Or enter a search word related to this book for a more general search.
3. Click on the **Fetch It** button.

FactHound will fetch the best sites for you!

Index